To Jackie,

Happy Reading!

THE BOY UNDER THE BED

BY PRESTON MCCLEAR --- ILLUSTRATIONS BY NICHOLAS DOLLAK

Preston McClear

3/26/02

FIFTH PRINTING

Copyright © 2000 by Malibu Books for Children

Published in the United States of America by Malibu Books for Children,
a division of Malibu Films, Inc.
48 Broad Street #134 Red Bank, NJ 07701
e-mail: MalibuInc@aol.com
Website: http://www.malibu-kids.com

Printed in Hong Kong

10 9 8 7 6

ISBN 1-929084-02-1

LCCN 00-104398

Jacket and book design by Nicholas Dollak

for my nephews,
Zane and Sean

Once Upon A Time,
in a bedroom not unlike yours and mine,
full of knick knacks, brick bracks & other snacks,
there lived a monster named Giles…

…with a boy under his bed.

Each night when the clock struck ten
the boy crawled out
and danced about.

Giles woke with a start,
then began to shout:
"FATHER, MOTHER,
COME QUICKLY! THE BOY IS OUT."

But boys are clever and disguise themselves well
so Father and Mother can never tell.

Mother and Father always say,
"Boys don't exist today."

But once the lights are turned out
that mischievous boy is at it again,
whooping, hollering and laughing.

Jumping from the dresser to the floor
and thumping against the door.

Wearing a sheet and saying,
"BOO TO YOU!!!"

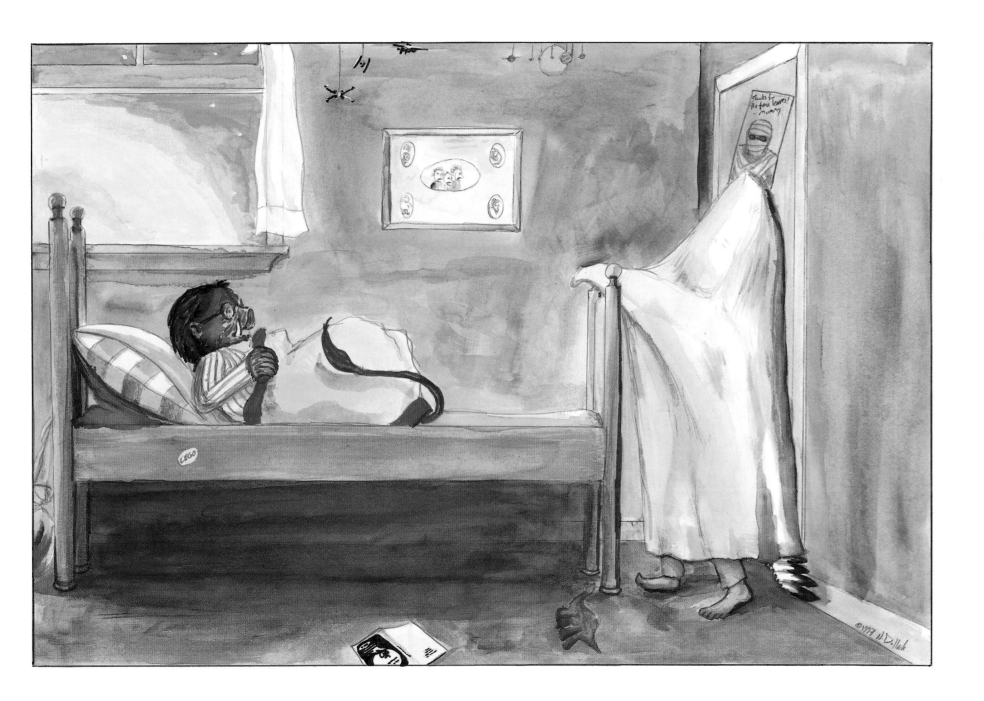

At the crack of dawn
the boy is always gone…

…Only to return once again
at the stroke of ten.

All through breakfast Mother and Father say again and again, "THERE ARE NO SUCH THINGS AS BOYS."

One night, while hiding under the covers,
Giles whispers a song:
"Bumper, Stumper… Go away, boy…
With a prayer of relief, the snap of my tail & the click of my feet,
you vanish, thief, from beneath,
so monster can sleep."

"OUCH!" a voice exclaims from under the bed.
"Careful with that prayer!
You've given me a knot on my head the size of a pear."

Standing up in bed, Giles cries:
"BE GONE… BE GONE FROM UNDER THERE,
BEFORE I SAY A DOZEN MORE OF THE SAME PRAYER."

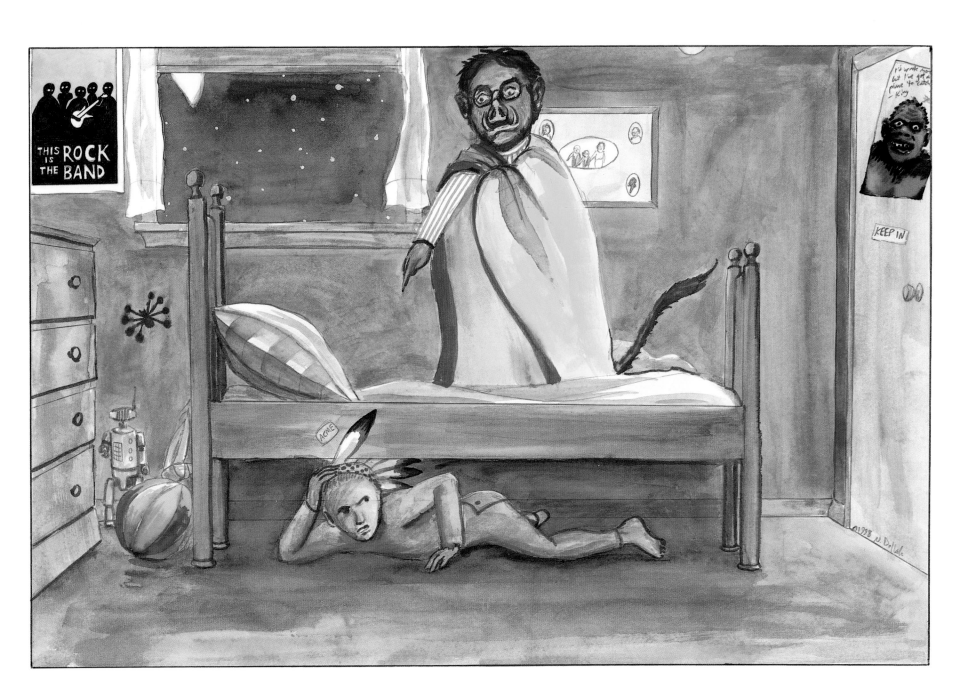

Crawling out from under the bed and rubbing his head,
the boy shouts, "You be gone."

Giles sings again, "Bumper, Stumper… Go away, boy…
With a prayer of relief, the snap of my tail & the click of my feet,
you vanish, thief, from beneath, so monster can sleep."

The boy replies, "Well, Monster, I'm sorry to say,
I've lost my way.
Won't you please let me stay?"

"NO… NO… BE GONE. BOYS LIE
SO THEY CAN MAKE MONSTER PIE."

Much to Giles' astonishment, the boy begins to cry.
Giles kneels down and whispers, "Why do you cry?"

"Because I'm alone and I can't find my way home.
I've also heard that monsters lie so they can make boy pie."

"Well, I've never had boy pie,
and I don't even think I'd like to try," says Giles.
"But I have a light, and it might help you find your way tonight."

Climbing into the corridor beneath the bed,
Giles and the boy follow the light…
Until rounding the bend they come to a door
marked #10.

"Well, this is it, my friend.
You've helped me find my way home again,"
says the boy. "You've been swell!
Won't you come in for a spell?"

Before Giles can protest, the boy whisks him
through door #10 into the secret den.

Passing… Passing through the door and clambering
up through the floor, emerging from under the bed,
Giles beholds with his eyes a mighty tree-house
perched in the skies.

With a whistle and a whoop, the boy announces his return.
"Well, lads, gather around the den and meet my new friend.
I was lost and he helped me find my way home again.
Come on; don't be afraid.
This monster is more fun than a parade!"

Soon there are boys… Boys crawling out of every corner and cranny. Some boys are dressed like cowboys, some boys are dressed like Indians; some are dressed like cops, some are dressed like robbers.

Some are tall, some are small.
Boys will be boys after all…

"Three cheers for my friend the monster!" shouts the boy.

Then, with a Hey and a Hoorah, one and all lift Giles from the floor. "THREE CHEERS! MONSTER IS HERE," they sing.
"TONIGHT YOU'LL BE OUR KING."

©1998 N. Dallah

The boy asks Giles, "O Mighty King,
what is the thing you decree?"

From his great throne, King Giles declares:
"TAG… YOU'RE IT!"

And so, beneath the moon,
in their Tree-House Room,
the children play
the evening away.

However, time waits for no boy or monster.
But in the evenings, boys and monsters are much the same;
all return again for fun and games.

Some evenings the boys visit Giles for a grand game of Cowboys and Indians.

On other nights, Giles and his friends visit the boys
for a game of Mad Scientists and Monsters.

And this, you see, is how monsters came
to be underneath boys' beds.

❖ THE END ❖